Snow White

First published in 2007 by
Franklin Watts
338 Euston Road
London
NW1 3BH

Franklin Watts Australia
Level 17/207 Kent Street
Sydney
NSW 2000

A CIP catalogue record for this book is available
from the British Library.

ISBN 978 0 7496 7074 0 (hbk)
ISBN 978 0 7496 7418 2 (pbk)

Series Editor: Melanie Palmer
Series Advisor: Dr Barrie Wade
Series Designer: Peter Scoulding

Printed in China

Franklin Watts is a division of Hachette Children's Books.

HOPSCOTCH
FAIRY TALES

Snow White

by Maggie Moore and The Pope Twins

W
FRANKLIN WATTS
LONDON•SYDNEY

Once there was a
princess named Snow White.

Snow White's stepmother, the queen, was beautiful but very vain.

She always asked her magic mirror:
"Mirror, mirror on the wall,
who's the fairest of them all?"

Every time the mirror replied:
"Queen, you are the fairest in
the land."

As Snow White grew older,
she grew more beautiful.

Then one day, when the queen asked her mirror who was the fairest of all, she got a shock.

The mirror told her:

"Snow White is the fairest

in the land."

The queen was furious. She
ordered a huntsman to take
Snow White into the forest
and kill her.

But the kind huntsman felt sorry
for Snow White and let her go.

Snow White ran far into the forest and found a little house. Seven dwarfs lived there.

Snow White stayed and looked after the house while the dwarfs worked. They were all very happy.

One day, the queen asked her
mirror again who was the fairest.
"Snow White is the fairest in the
land," it still replied.

The queen realised that the
huntsman had tricked her.
She quickly sent her spies to
find Snow White.

When the queen found out where Snow White was hiding, she decided to get rid of Snow White herself.

First, she dressed up as an old woman and went to the little house to trick Snow White.

The queen tied ribbons so
tightly around Snow White's
waist that she could not breathe.

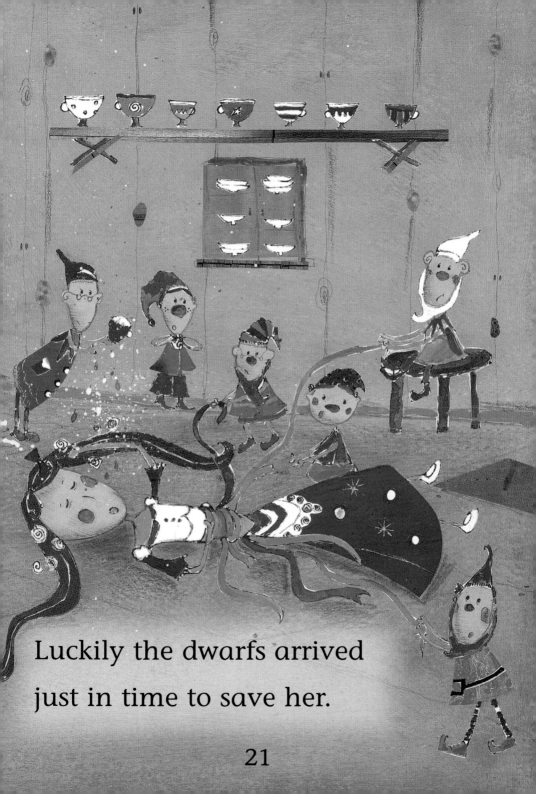

Luckily the dwarfs arrived
just in time to save her.

Next, the queen sold Snow White a poisoned comb and pushed it into her hair.

Again the dwarfs found her before it was too late.

Finally, the queen tricked
Snow White into eating a
poisoned apple.

But this time the dwarfs were too
late. They put Snow White into
a glass case and looked after her.

The next day, a prince rode by and saw Snow White in the glass case. He thought she was the most beautiful girl he had ever seen.

He wanted to take Snow White
to his palace.

As the prince's men lifted Snow White from the case, the apple fell from her throat. She sat up and saw the prince.

They fell in love at once!

Snow White and the prince invited the wicked queen to their wedding. But the queen was so angry that she ran away and was never seen again.

Hopscotch has been specially designed to fit the requirements of the National Literacy Strategy. It offers real books by top authors and illustrators for children developing their reading skills. There are 43 Hopscotch stories to choose from:

* hardback